Enid Blyton's

CHRISTMAS TALES

A Templar Book
This edition published in the USA in 1993 by
SMITHMARK Publishers Inc, 16 East 32nd Street, New York, New York 10016

SMITHMARK books are available for bulk purchase for sales promotion
and premium use. For details write or telephone the Manager of Special Sales,
SMITHMARK Publishers Inc, 16 East 32nd Street, New York, New York 10016;
(212) 532-6600

This edition published in Canada by Smithbooks,
113 Merton Street, Toronto, Canada M45 1A8

Produced by The Templar Company plc,
Pippbrook Mill, London Road, Dorking, Surrey RH4 1JE, Great Britain

Illustrated by Shirley Willis and Sue Deakin

Printed and bound in Singapore

ISBN 0-8317-1272-4

Enid Blyton's
CHRISTMAS TALES

SMITHMARK

CONTENTS

The Night the Toys Came to Life

It was Christmas Eve and the nursery was very, very quiet. Sarah and Jack had gone to bed. All their toys were shut up safely in the big toy cupboard. Nothing could be heard but the ticking of the cuckoo-clock on the wall.

The cuckoo-bird suddenly popped out of the clock, flapped her wooden wings, and cried "Cuckoo!" twelve times. It was twelve o'clock, the middle of the night.

Now, one toy had been left out of the toy cupboard, just one. It was Teddy, the big brown teddy bear. He had one glass eye, and one boot-button eye. Once he had lost a glass eye, so Sarah had sewn on a button instead, and he said he could see quite well with it. Right now, Teddy was asleep, but the cuckoo woke him up with a jump.

"Who is playing hide-and-seek?" cried Teddy.

The cuckoo laughed and popped her head out of the clock-door again.

"No one," she said. "I was cuckooing twelve o'clock, that's all. Teddy, you have been left out of the cupboard! Put the light on and let all the other toys out, and have a party!"

"Oooh yes!" said Teddy. So up he got, climbed on to a chair and switched on the light. Then he ran across to the toy cupboard. He turned the key – click – and the cupboard door opened!

"Come out, toys, come out!" cried Teddy.

All the toys woke up with a jump. "Who is that calling us?" they cried. "Oh, it's you, Teddy. Can we really come out of the toy cupboard? Oh, what fun!"

Then out came the curly-haired doll, very grand in a pink silk dress. Behind came the small teddy bear with his red hat and red sweater. Then came the jack-in-the-box, the little wind-up mouse, and the wind-up clown, tumbling head-over-heels. Two toy cars came next, and then all the skittles, hopping on tiny legs. The skittle-ball went with them, but he behaved well, and didn't knock the skittles down.

The pink cat and blue dog came together. They were great friends. The wind-up train puffed out, and ran all around the nursery in excitement. And Rag Doll floated down from the top of the cupboard, hanging onto her parasol, so she wouldn't land on the floor with a big bump.

"Hurry, hurry!" said Teddy. "Don't take all night walking out! We want to have some fun, and there won't be very much time."

"What shall we do?" said the curly-haired doll. "Let's do something exciting! Let's have a Christmas party?"

"Oh, yes, yes!" cried all the toys, and Teddy gave such a shout of delight that he frightened the wind-up mouse.

"I'll make some cakes on the toy stove!" said Teddy. "I'm good at that." And he started to work.

"Pink Cat and I will go to the toy candy store," said the blue dog. "There is lots of candy there. We will take some out of the jars and put them on little plates. Everyone will like those."

"There is a pitcher of milk on the table," said the rag doll. "I will get it, and we will fill the toy tea-pot with milk, and pretend it is tea."

Rag Doll and Teddy got the pitcher safely down on the floor. The pink cat popped her head into the pitcher and took a lick. "Very nice and creamy," she said. "Oh, Teddy, how delicious your cakes smell! Open the oven door and see if they are nearly ready."

The teddy opened the little oven door, and took out the pan of cakes. They were lovely – warm and brown, smelling most delicious. "They are just ready," called Teddy.

"We had better dress ourselves up for the party," said Jack-in-the-Box. "I shall put on a new hat and polish up my brass buttons a bit."

Everyone hurried to make themselves nice for the party. The curly-haired doll brushed her hair out till it was like a cloud round her face.

She tied it up
with a blue ribbon.
The pink cat got the blue
dog to tie a fine bow around
her neck, and she tied a blue
bow around the blue dog's tail.
He looked very smart.
    Even the wind-up
mouse got Small Bear to
tie a sash around his fat little
middle. "We want bows, too,"
said the skittles, but there
was no more ribbon left.
"You look quite smart in
your red uniform," said the
wind-up mouse.

"Let's ask the dolls' house dolls too!" said Teddy.
"I am sure they would like to come!" So he knocked at the
front door of the dolls' house, and the little Mother-
doll opened it. She was so pleased when she heard there
was to be a party. "I and Daddy-doll, and all the little
children-dolls would love to come!" she said.

So they all ran out of the dolls' house in their best
dresses and suits, looking as sweet as could be.

"Now we will begin the party," said Teddy. "What shall
we sit on? There are only two dolls' chairs."

"We can each sit on a block!" said the blue dog. "I will

get them out of the block-box." The pink cat helped him to bring out the big wooden blocks, and they set them all around the little table. The curly-haired doll had already put a pretty cloth on it, and had arranged all the cups and saucers and plates from the toy tea-set. She had filled the big tea-pot with milk.

"I want to pour, I want to pour!" said the wind-up mouse. But the doll wouldn't let him. "You would spill the tea," she said. "Go and sit down like a good mouse."

Even the big rocking-horse rocked up to join the party. He chewed up four of Teddy's cakes in no time and he drank fourteen cups of tea – though really it was milk, of course.

"Your cakes are delicious, Teddy!" said the rag doll, and the bear blushed bright red with pride. He looked quite funny for a minute, but he soon became his usual color again. It really was a lovely party.

"Has everyone had enough to eat?" asked Teddy at last. "There isn't anything left – not even a piece of candy, and the tea-pot is empty. What shall we do now?"

"Play games and dance!" cried the blue dog. "Let's play tag! I'll catch you, Small Bear, I'll catch you!" The small teddy bear gave a squeal and ran away. The wind-up clown went head-over-heels as fast as ever he could, and upset all the skittles.

Bang-smack-bang! Down they went with such a noise. The wind-up mouse squealed loudly when one skittle fell on top of him.

"I feel like singing," said the pink cat suddenly. "I want to sing." So she opened her mouth and sang loudly, but nobody liked her song at all. "It's nothing but 'Meow, meow, meow'!" said the curly-haired doll. "Do stop, Pink Cat."

"I want to dance!" cried a big skittle. "We skittles can dance beautifully. We want some music."

"Well, start the music box then," said Teddy.
"I'll wind the handle. Are you ready?" And then
the nursery was suddenly full of loud tinkling music
as the teddy turned the handle of the music box.
What a noise there was!

Now, outside in the street, the night watchman was going on his rounds, with his flashlight in his hand. He was shining it on to people's front-doors to make sure they were closed tight. He was a very good night watchman indeed.

Suddenly he came to a stop. "I hear a strange noise!" he said. "What can it be? It is music playing! It is people squealing and laughing. It is somebody singing a loud Meow song. How very strange in the middle of the night – even if it is the night before Christmas!"

He listened for a little while, and then he made up his mind to find out what all the noise was about. "I am sure the people of the house are all in bed!" he said. "Ho! Who can it be making all this dreadful noise? I must certainly stop it."

Now the toys hadn't heard the night watchman walking by outside, because they were making such a noise. Suddenly they heard a knocking at the window! "Oooh, what's that?" cried Teddy in a fright. "Turn out the light, quickly!"

So the curly-haired doll switched off the light — and then, in at the window shone the night watchman's flashlight. Oh, what a fright the toys got! "Save me, save me!" cried the wind-up mouse and bumped into all the skittles and knocked them down, clitter-clatter, clitter-clatter.

"What's going on here?" said the deep voice of the night watchman, and he climbed in the window. He shone his light all around the nursery. "What, nobody here but toys?" he said in great surprise. "Then what could that noise have been?"

"Please, it was us," said the teddy, in a very small voice. The night watchman was so astonished when he heard the teddy speaking to him that he couldn't say a word.

"You see, we were having a party," said the curly-haired doll, and she switched on the light again. Then the night watchman saw the remains of the party on the table. "Teddy baked some cakes, and the pink cat got some candy from the toy candy store," said the doll.

"Oh, what a pity I didn't come a little sooner," said the big night watchman. "I could have had a cake then. I get so hungry in the middle of the night."

"I'll make you some!" cried Teddy, hurrying to the toy stove. "Have a ride on the rocking-horse while the cakes are baking. They won't take long!"

So the night watchman got on to the rocking-horse, and the horse gave him a fine ride while the cakes were cooking.

The teddy bear baked a beautiful batch of cakes. The pink cat filled a little dish with more candy from the shop. The curly-haired doll tipped up the big pitcher and filled the tea-pot once more. The dolls' house mother-doll took a cup and saucer and plate into the dolls' house and washed it for the night watchman.

Suddenly something happened! The kitchen cat came creeping in at the door, for she had heard all the noise too. She stood there looking at the busy toys – and she suddenly saw the wind-up mouse rushing across the floor!

"A mouse, a mouse!" she mewed, and she pounced on the frightened mouse at once. The mouse's key flew out of his side, and he gave a loud squeal. "Let the mouse go!" cried Teddy. "Bad cat!" shouted the wind-up clown.

But the cat would not let the poor little mouse go. Then the big night watchman got off the rocking-horse and walked over to the cat. He took out his black notebook and a big pencil.

"I must have your name and address," he said to the surprised cat. "I must report you for cruelty to animals. See how you have frightened this poor little mouse!"

The cat fled away in fright. The toys crowded around the night watchman. "Oh, thank you, thank you, kind Night Watchman!" they cried.

"You are so kind," said the clockwork mouse, rubbing his little nose against the night watchman's boots. "I wish you were my very own night watchman. I do like you!"

S.W.

"Come and eat my cakes," said Teddy. The night watchman looked at them. "Dear me!" he said. "I shall never be able to eat all those! Can't we ask someone else to come and share them with me?"

"Let's ask Sarah and Jack!" cried Teddy. "They are asleep, but we can soon wake them."

"You go," said the rag doll. "Tell them we want them to share in our fun. They are nice children and have always been kind to us. It would be fun to share the party with them."

So the teddy went out of the door and tiptoed to the children's room. He climbed up on to the bed and pulled at the sheet. "Wake up," he said, "wake up. There's a party going on!"

Sarah and Jack woke up. They *were* surprised to see Teddy. "Have you come alive?" they said. "Of course I have," said Teddy. "Do hurry up and come to the party!"

So the two children put on their robes and slippers, and went to share the toys' party. They couldn't help feeling very excited.

"Here they come, here they come!" said the toys to one another. "Hello, Sarah; hello, Jack!"

The two children walked into the nursery and were most surprised to see all the toys running around, and the skittles hopping, and the two cars rushing over the carpet.

But they were even more surprised to see the big night watchman. "Good gracious!" said Sarah, staring at him. "What are you doing in our nursery in the middle of the night?"

The night watchman told them. "I heard such a noise in here, and I came to see what the matter was," he said. "Then the toys kindly invited me to their party. But the teddy bear made so many cakes that I knew I couldn't eat them all myself. So he went to get you two."

"Oh, how lovely!" said Sarah. "Teddy, I didn't know you could make cakes. You never said a word about it!"

Teddy bowed low and went very red again. He couldn't help feeling very proud. "Please sit down on the floor," he said, "and I and the dolls will wait on you. It is a great honor to have you and the big night watchman at our party!"

So the two children and the night watchman sat down on the floor, and all the toys waited on them. "Will you have a cup of tea?" asked the curly-haired doll, handing a full cup and saucer to Sarah. "It's really only milk," she said in a whisper.

"It tastes *just* like tea," said Sarah, and she drank out of the tiny cup.

"Will you have one of my cakes?" said Teddy, and offered a plate of his little brown cakes. The children thought they were simply delicious. They crunched them up at once and told the teddy bear that they had never tasted such lovely cakes before. This time Teddy went purple with pride, and the wind-up mouse stared at him in surprise. "Did you know you were purple?" he asked. "You do look funny, Teddy."

The night watchman ate a big meal too – in fact he ate twenty-three of Teddy's cakes, and a whole plate of candy. He drank sixteen cups of tea, which was even more than the rocking-horse had had.

It was a lovely meal, except when the rocking-horse came too near and nibbled some of the night watchman's hair off. That made him rather cross and he took out his notebook again. The rocking-horse was afraid of being asked to give his name and address so he moved away quickly.

"Now what shall we do?" asked Sarah, when they had eaten all the cakes and candy. "We can't very well play games with you toys, because we are rather too big, and we should make such a noise."

"We will give a fine show for you!" said Small Bear. "We will set the music box going, and the curly-haired doll shall dance her best dance. She really does dance beautifully!"

So the curly-haired doll danced her best dance to the
music, and everyone clapped their hands. Then the
wind-up clown showed how well he could knock down all
the skittles by going head-over-heels, but the skittles were
tired of that and they chased the clown all around the
nursery. He got into the block-box and the skittles locked
him in there for almost ten minutes. That made the
children laugh.

Then the two cars ran a race with the wind-up train and that was great fun. They all bumped into one another and fell over at the end, so nobody knew who won. Then Small Bear stood on his head and waved his feet in the air. Everybody thought he was very clever. "Can you do that, Night Watchman?" asked Teddy.

"I don't know. I'll try," said the big night watchman, and he got up. But he couldn't do tricks like Small Bear.

He soon sat down again, and mopped his head with a big red handkerchief. "I'd rather watch you do tricks than try them myself," he said. "Hallo – what's this?"

The night watchman and the children saw that the toy farm had suddenly come to life. It stood in a corner of the nursery, and nobody had thought of waking up the farmer, his wife, and animals. But they had heard the noise of the party, and now they were all very lively indeed!

"The ducks are swimming on the pond!" said Sarah.

"The cows are nibbling the toy grass," said Jack.

"The hens are laying little eggs!" said the night watchman in surprise. "And look at those tiny lambs frisking about! There goes the farmer to milk his cows. Well, well, well – it's a wonderful sight to see!"

The toy farm-dog barked around the sheep. The toy horse dragged the toy farm-cart along. The toy pigs grunted and rooted about in their little toy sty. The children really loved watching everything.

"Oh!" said Sarah. "I have always, always wanted our toy farm to come alive – and now it has. Jack, isn't it lovely? Oh, do look – the farmer's wife is offering us a tiny, tiny egg!" So she was. The night watchman and the two children took one each. They were very pleased.

Just as they were all watching the toy farm, a loud noise made everyone jump. It was the toy rooster on the farm, crowing as loudly as he could.

"Cock-a-doodle-doo! Cock-a-doodle-doo!"

"It's day-break!" cried Teddy, in surprise. "How quickly the time has gone."

"It's dawn!" cried the curly-haired doll. "The sun will soon be up. Time for all toys to go back to the cupboard. Hurry now, hurry!

"We must not be alive after day-break. Hurry, toys!"

Then what a hurry-scurry there was for the toy cupboard! The night watchman and the children watched in surprise. The skittles hopped in. The wind-up mouse tore in at top speed. The wind-up clown went head-over-heels right into the back of the cupboard. The pink cat and blue dog ran together, their whiskers touching. Teddy put the blocks into the box quickly. The dolls' house dolls cleared away the party-things, and then ran to their house and shut the front door.

"Good-night – or rather, good-morning!" said Teddy, popping his head out of the cupboard. "So glad you came and shared our fun! Good-bye – and come again another day!"

"Well, that's all over," said Sarah, with a sigh. "Oh, wasn't it fun? Did you enjoy it too, Night Watchman?"

"I should think I did," said the night watchman. "Well, I must be getting back to my work, or somebody will be after me. And you two had better go to bed. I'll get out of the window. Good-night and Merry Christmas!"

"Merry Christmas!" said Sarah and Jack. They watched the night watchman get out of the window and then they went to the nursery door. "Good-night, toys," they said softly.

And out of the toy cupboard came a crowd of tiny voices, from the little growl of Small Bear to the squeak of the wind-up mouse. "Good-night, Sarah and Jack, good-night and Merry Christmas!"

Then Teddy poked his head out of the cupboard again. "It was all because you didn't put me away in the cupboard tonight that the party happened!" he said. "Leave me out again sometime, please!"

"We will!" said the children. What fun they'll have when they do!

Santa's Workshop

I n the nursery all the toys were getting ready for Christmas. The dolls' house dolls were making paper chains, the wind-up sailor was baking mince pies, even Panda was helping to make decorations, and he had only arrived in the nursery three weeks before – a present from the children's Aunt Jane.

All the toys were helping, except for one – the big rocking-horse that lived in the middle of the nursery floor. He was a fine fellow with a lovely spotted coat, a big mane, and a bushy black tail.

He rocked back and forth and took the children for long rides around the nursery floor. They all loved him – but the toys were afraid of him.

Sometimes he would begin to rock when they were playing around, and then, how they ran out of the way!

Sometimes he was so proud and so vain that he would not play with the other nursery toys.

"I'm too important to do boring things like making paper chains," he boasted. "I'm the only toy in this nursery big enough for the children to ride on. I ought to be king of the nursery for Christmas."

"Well, you don't deserve to be," said the curly-haired doll. "You squashed the monkey's tail yesterday, and that was unkind."

"I didn't mean to," said the horse, offended. "He shouldn't have left it lying around under my rockers. Silly of him."

"You should have looked down before you began to rock, and you would have seen it," said the doll.

"Well! Do you suppose I'm going to bother to look for tails and things before I begin to rock?" said the horse. "You just look out for yourselves! That's the best thing to do."

But the toys were careless. Later that morning the little red toy car ran under the horse's rockers and had his paint badly scratched. Next, the wind-up sailor left his key there and the rocking-horse bent it when he rocked on it. It was difficult to wind up the sailor after that, and he was cross.

Then the curly-haired doll dropped her bead necklace and the rocking-horse rocked on it and smashed some of the beads. The toys were really upset with him about that.

"Be careful, be careful!" they cried. "Tell us before you rock, Rocking-horse! You might rock on one of us and hurt us badly!"

But the rocking-horse just laughed and thought it was a great joke to scare the toys so much.

"You are not kind," said Ben the big teddy bear.

"One day you will be sorry."

And so he was, as you will hear.

It happened that, on the day before Christmas, Sarah and Jack had been playing with their toys and had left them all around the nursery when they had gone for lunch.

Now, the panda's head, and one of his ears were just under the rocker of the rocking-horse. And as soon as the children had left the room the rocking-horse decided to rock.

"Stop! Stop!" shrieked the toys, running forward. "Panda is underneath!"

But the rocking-horse didn't listen. No, he thought the toys were scared as usual, and he didn't listen to what they said. Back and forth he rocked – and poor Panda was underneath!

Oh dear, oh dear, when the toys got to him what a sight he was! Some of his nice black fur had come out, and his right ear was all squashed. The toys pulled him away and began to cry.

"What's the matter?" asked the rocking-horse, stopping and looking down.

"You naughty horse! We told you to stop! Now see what you have done!" cried the toys angrily. "You are really very unkind. We won't speak to you or play with you any more."

"Don't then," said the horse, and he rocked away by himself. "Cree-eek, cree-eek! I'm sure I don't want to talk to you or give you rides if you are going to be so cross with me."

S.H.P.

After that the toys paid no attention to the naughty rocking-horse.

They made a great fuss over Panda, who soon stopped crying. Then they went on getting ready for Christmas. Ben wrapped up a present for the pink cat, Rag Doll made a Christmas stocking, and Jack-in-the-Box helped the other toys hang tinsel on the Christmas tree. They had such fun!

In the corner of the nursery, Rocking-horse felt sad. He usually helped hang the tinsel because he could reach higher than the other toys.

"I wish they'd talk to me!" he thought to himself. "I wish they'd play. I'd like to give them each a ride around the nursery – in fact, I'd take three of them at once if they asked me."

But the toys acted as if the rocking-horse wasn't there at all. They didn't ask him to help with anything. They didn't even look at him.

"He's unkind and selfish and horrid," they said.
"And the best way to treat people like that is not to
pay any attention to them."

So the rocking-horse got sadder and sadder, and
longed to gallop around the nursery just for a change.
But he was afraid the toys might be cross if he did.

Now, just as it was getting dark the children's
puppy came into the nursery, because someone
had left the door open. The toys fled to the
toy cupboard in fear, because the puppy
was very playful and liked to carry
a toy outdoors and chew it.

Everyone got
safely into the cupboard
except the pink cat. She slipped
and fell, and the puppy pounced on her.
He chewed and nibbled her whiskers clean
away! Nobody dared to rescue her, not even the
rocking-horse, though he did wonder if he should
gallop at the puppy.

Then somebody whistled from downstairs, and the
puppy flew out of the door.

The poor pink cat sat up.

"Oh!" she said. "Whatever has happened to my fine pink whiskers?"

"They've gone," said Panda, peeping out of the cupboard. "The puppy has chewed them off. There they are, look, on the floor, in tiny little bits."

The pink cat cried bitterly. She had been proud of her whiskers. "A cat doesn't look like cat without her whiskers," she wept.

The sound of the pink cat crying made Panda feel so sad that soon he was crying too.

"What shall we do?" he wailed. "Oh, what shall we do? When Sarah and Jack see us, all nibbled and squashed, they will throw us into the dustbin. Boo-hoo-hoo!"

"Yes," sobbed the pink cat. "They won't want us if they are given brand-new toys for Christmas." And before long the nursery was filled with the sound of toys crying.

How the rocking-horse wished he had not been so unkind! He would miss any of the toys terribly if they were thrown away – and it would be mostly his fault, too! Whatever could he do to earn their forgiveness? He looked around the nursery at all the Christmas decorations and suddenly he knew just what to do.

"Excuse me, toys – but I've got an idea," he said in his humblest voice.

"It's only the rocking-horse," said Ben. "Don't pay any attention to him."

"Please do pay some attention," said the horse. "I've got a good idea. I can take all the broken toys to Santa Claus's workshop. I know the way because I came from there. Perhaps Santa Claus can fix you all and make you better?"

"But it's Christmas Eve!" cried Panda. "Santa will be too busy delivering presents to have time for *us*."

"Oh no!" replied Rocking-horse. "Santa is the friend of every old toy. No matter how busy he is, I'm sure he will find time to help us if we ask him tonight!"

"Well! Let's go then," said the teddy bear. So the toys helped Pink Cat and Panda, Wind-up Sailor and the monkey, Curly-haired Doll and the little red toy car all up on to Rocking-horse's back. Then Ben sat at the very front and said,

"Let's go!"

"Cree-eek, cree-eek!" went Rocking-horse, across the nursery floor and up, away out of the window and into the night sky. For miles and miles they travelled, rocking past twinkling stars towards the great hill where Santa Claus lived.

Luckily for the toys, Santa was at home. He was busy piling a new load of presents onto his magic sleigh. His faithful reindeer would take them fast and far – to the other side of the world in the blink of an eye. When he heard the sound of the rocking-horse neighing and hrrumphing at the door, he came to see who was there.

Rocking-horse explained why they had come and, to the toys' delight, Santa said he would be glad to help. He only had three more loads to deliver before morning. Then he inspected each of the toys in turn to see what the damage was.

"Dear, dear!" said Santa Claus, looking severely at the rocking-horse. "I hope you are ashamed of yourself. I have heard of you and your stupid ways of scaring the toys by rocking suddenly when they are near. Come in!"

The horse rocked in and followed Santa Claus to his workshop. In no time at all Santa had straightened out Wind-up Sailor's key and mended the curly-haired doll's broken beads. He soon fixed the monkey's squashed tail and patched up the toy car's scratched paint.

Then it was Panda's turn. Santa opened a drawer and looked into it.

"Dear me!" he said. "I've no panda fur left. It's all been used up. Now what am I to do?"

He turned and looked at the rocking-horse.

"You've a nice thick black mane!" he said. "I think you'll have to spare a little for Panda!"

Then, to the rocking-horse's horror, he took out a pair of scissors and cut a patch out of his thick mane! How strange it looked!

Quickly and neatly, Santa Claus put the black fur on to the panda's head. He stuck it there with glue, and it soon dried. Then Santa looked at Panda's squashed ear.

He found a new ear and carefully put it on. It belonged to a teddy bear, really, so it was brown, instead of black, and looked rather odd.

"Now I've no special black paint!" said Santa in a vexed tone. "Only blue or red. That won't do for a panda's ear. Ha, I'll have to take off one of your nice black spots, Rocking-horse, and use it for the panda's ear. That will do nicely!"

He carefully scraped off a large spot on the horse's back, mixed it with a tiny drop of water and then painted it on Panda's new ear. It looked fine!

"Thank you very much indeed!" said the panda, gratefully. "You are very kind."

"Not at all!" said Santa, beaming all over his big, kind face. "I'm always ready to help toys, you know! And how can I help you?" he said, looking at the pink cat. She soon explained all about her whiskers.

"Oh dear, oh dear, oh dear!" said Santa shaking his head sadly. "I'm right out of whiskers."

Just then, a small voice piped up behind him. It was Rocking-horse.

"I should be very pleased to give the toy cat some of the hairs out of my long black tail," he said. "They would do beautifully for whiskers."

"But how can we get them out?" said the pink cat.

"Pull them out, of course," said the horse.

"But it will hurt you," said the pink cat.

"I don't mind," said the horse, bravely. "Pull as many as you like!" So Santa pulled eight out, and they did hurt. But the horse didn't make a sound.

Then Santa carefully gave the cat her whiskers back.

"One whisker!" he said. "Two whiskers! Three whiskers! Oh, you will look fine when I have finished, Pink Cat. These are black whiskers, long and strong, and you will look very handsome now." And so she did. Very fine indeed!

At last it was time to go, so all the toys clambered back on to the rocking-horse.

"Thank you Santa," they cried as they left. "Thank you for helping us all."

Then off they went home again, rocking hard all the way in order to get home by morning, and glad to be good as new again.

The toys cheered when they saw them.

"What glorious fur you have – and look at your fine new ear!" they cried when they saw Panda. "And look at your lovely whiskers," they said to Pink Cat.

Rocking-horse said nothing. He stood in the middle of the nursery floor, quite still, not a rock left in him.

"Santa took some of Rocking-horse's hair for me, and one of his spots to paint my ear black," said Panda. "You can see where he has a bare place on his mane, and one of his biggest spots is missing."

Sure enough, it was just as Panda had said.

"I must say it was nice of the rocking-horse to give you them," said Ben, suddenly.

"And to give me my new whiskers," added Pink Cat. "Especially as we haven't even spoken to him lately. Very nice of him."

All the other toys thought the same. So, they went over to the rocking-horse who was still looking sad.

"Thank you for taking us to Santa's workshop," said the curly-haired doll.

"It was very kind of you," said the monkey.

"I can't thank you enough!" said the pink cat. "I had pink whiskers before, and they didn't show up very well – but these show beautifully. Don't you think so?"

"You look very handsome," said the horse. "Very!"

"Your tail looks a bit thin now, I'm afraid," said the pink cat. "Do you mind?"

"Not a bit," said the rocking-horse. "I can rock back and forth just as fast when my tail is thin as when it's thick. You get on my back and see, Pink Cat!"

So up got the pink cat, and the rocking-horse went rocking around the nursery at top speed. It was very exciting. You may be sure the horse looked where he was going this time! He wasn't going to rock over anyone's tail again!

"Oh, thank you!" said the pink cat, quite out of breath. "That was the nicest ride I ever had!"

"Anyone can have one!" said the horse, rather gruffly, because he was afraid that the toys might say "No," and turn their backs on him.

But they didn't. They all climbed up at once.

"Nice old horse!" they said. "We're friends again now, aren't we? Gallop away, gallop away!"

And you should have seen him gallop away again, around and around the nursery until the sun peeped through the curtains.

"Merry Christmas, Merry Christmas," they heard the children shouting.

"Good gracious," said Ben the teddy bear. "It's Christmas Day!" All the toys had quite forgotten.

And a lovely Christmas Day it turned out to be, too. Sarah and Jack were amazed at how smart all their old toys looked – apart from Rocking-horse, whose mane and tail looked a bit straggly.

"Never mind," said Sarah. "We will always love you, toys, even if you are old and worn, won't we Jack?"

"Oh yes," said Jack. "Merry Christmas toys. Merry Christmas to you all!"

Christmas in the Toyshop

Once upon a time there was a toy shop. It sold candy as well as toys, so it was a very nice shop indeed.

All the children loved it. They used to come each day and press their noses against the window, and look in to see what toys there were.

"Oh look at that beautiful doll!" they would say. "Oh, do you see that train with its three cars – and it's got tracks to run on too."

"Look at the rocking-horse. I do love his friendly face!"

"Oh, what a lovely shop this is! When we grow up let's have a shop *just* like this one!"

Miss Roundy, the shopkeeper, liked having a toy shop. She liked seeing the children and showing them all her toys, and she nearly always gave them an extra candy or two in their bags when they came to spend their pocket money. So, of course, the children all loved her.

The toys loved her, too.

"Look – she found me a new key when mine dropped behind the shelf and couldn't be found," said the wind-up train.

"And she put a spot of red paint on my coat where some got rubbed off," said one of the toy soldiers. "She's very, very kind."

The toys liked living in Miss Roundy's shop until they were bought by the children. It was fun to sit on the shelves and the counter and watch the boys and girls come in and hear them talk. And it was very exciting when one of them was bought and taken proudly away by a child.

The toys didn't like Sundays as much as weekdays, because then the shop was closed, and nobody came to see them at all. They couldn't bear it when Miss Roundy took her summer vacation and closed the shop for two whole weeks! That was dreadful.

"It's so *dull*," complained the biggest teddy bear, and he pressed his middle to make himself growl mournfully. "There's no one to see and nothing to do. Miss Roundy even pulls down the window shade so that we can't see the children looking in at us."

And then Christmas time came, and the toys had a shock. Miss Roundy was going to close the shop for four whole days and go away to stay with her aunt. Oh dear!

"Four days of dullness and quietness and darkness," said the rocking horse, gloomily. "Nothing to do. No one to come and buy us, or see how nice we are. Four whole days!"

A black monkey with a red ribbon around his neck

spoke in a high, chattering voice.

"Can't we have a Christmas party for ourselves?"

"It's an idea," said the rocking horse, smiling. "Let's all think about it until Christmas comes – then we'll have a GRAND time in here by ourselves!"

The day came when Miss Roundy was going to close the shop. She pulled down the big window shade. Then she turned to the watching toys.

"I'm going now, toys," she said. "I won't see you again for four whole days. Be good. Merry Christmas to you – and try and have a good time yourselves. Do what you like – *I* won't mind! Merry Christmas!"

She went out of the shop and locked the door. The toys heard her foot-steps going down the street.

"Merry Christmas, Miss Roundy!" said everyone, softly. "You're nice!"

And now they were all alone for four days. *What* were they going to do?

The toys did what they always did as soon as the shop was closed for the night. They got up and stretched themselves, because they got stiff with sitting so long on the shelves and counter.

"That's better," said the rag doll, shaking out her legs one after the other to loosen them.

The pink cat rolled over and over. "Ah – that was good," she said, standing up again. "I love a roll."

The little wind-up train whistled loudly and the toy soldiers climbed out of their boxes and began marching back and forth.

"Nice to stretch our legs a little," they said, and then they scattered because the roly-poly man came rolling along, not looking where he was going, as usual.

"Look out," cried the captain of the soldiers, "you'll bump into the doll house! There he goes, rolling here and there – what a way to get around!"

"Listen, everyone!" called the rocking horse. "Let's talk about Christmas."

"When is it?" asked the big teddy bear.

"The day after tomorrow," said the rocking horse. "I think if we're going to have a good Christmas ourselves, we ought to make our plans now and get everything going, so that we're ready by Christmas Day."

"Oh yes!" cried everyone, and they all gathered around the rocking horse. What a crowd there was. All the little doll house dolls, and the other bigger dolls, the skittles, the wind-up train with its cars, and another wooden train, and the roly-poly man, and … well, I couldn't possibly tell you all of them, but you know what toys there are in a toy shop, don't you?

"Sit down," said the rocking horse. And everyone sat, except, of course, the things that could only stand, like the trains and the motor cars and the balls.

"We want a party," said the rocking horse. "That means we must have things to eat. We can take as much of the candy as we like, to make into cakes and things – Miss Roundy said we could help ourselves."

"We can make the food," said the doll house dolls.

"We'll help," said the skittles, excitedly.

"We can cook on that nice toy stove over there," said the twin dolls. One of the twins was a boy doll and the other was a girl doll, and they were exactly alike.

"The pink cat and the black monkey can arrange the circus," said the rocking horse. "They'll have lots of fun working together on that."

"I'll do the Christmas tree," said the wind-up sailor. "We'll have presents for everyone under it! We'll play games afterwards, too."

"What a pity Santa Claus doesn't know about us!" said the roly-poly man. "It would be so nice if he came to the party."

"I don't suppose he'll be able to come," said the black monkey. "He's much too busy at Christmas time. Don't roll against me like that, roly-poly man. You'll knock me over."

The roly-poly man rolled away and bumped into a row of soldiers. They went down on the floor at once. As they got up and brushed themselves off, they shouted angrily at the roly-poly man.

"Let's not quarrel," said the rocking horse. "People should never quarrel at Christmas time. It's a time to make one another happy and glad. Now – to your work, everyone – and we'll see what a wonderful Christmas Day we will have!"

The dolls and the skittles went to work at once. The doll with golden hair and the twin dolls took charge of the cooking. They got the little toy stove going, and there was soon a *most* delicious smell in the toy shop – the cakes were baking!

There were chocolate cakes and fudge cakes and peppermints. There were little jellies made of the jelly candy Miss Roundy sold. There was a very big iced cake with tiny candles on it that the rag doll had found in a box.

The baking and cooking went on all day long. The twin dolls had to scold the roly-poly man many times because he kept rolling against the golden-haired doll just as she was taking the cakes out of the oven.

Still, as you can see, there was plenty of everything.

"What a feast we are going to have!" said the rag doll, greedily. "Ooooh – fudge cakes – I'll have six of those, please, on Christmas Day!"

The wind-up sailor did the Christmas tree. He was very, very clever. He climbed right up to the highest shelf, which Miss Roundy had decorated with evergreens, and he chose a very nice piece of fir.

"Look out!" he called. "I'm going to push it off the shelf." So everyone looked out, and down came the little branch of fir tree, flopping down to the floor.

The wind-up sailor climbed down. He did a little dance of joy when he saw what a wonderful tree the bit of fir would make. He wondered what to put it in.

"If you'll get me out of my box, so that I can join in the fun for once, you can use my box," said the gruff voice of Jack-in-the-Box.

The toys didn't really like Jack-in-the-Box very much. He lived inside a square box, and when the box was opened he suddenly leaped out on a long spring, and frightened them very much. The wind-up sailor didn't really know if he wanted to get Jack out of his box.

"Come on – just this once,"
said Jack-in-the-Box.
"I promise to be good.
I'll perform in the circus,
and be funny if you like."
So Jack-in-the-Box
was taken out of his box
and he wobbled everywhere
on his long spring, enjoying
his freedom very much.

The box was just right for the Christmas tree. The wind-up sailor filled it with dirt that he took from the pot that held a big plant belonging to Miss Roundy. Then he planted the piece of fir tree in it.

"Now to decorate it!" he said. So he got some tiny colored candles and some bright beads out of the bead box, and some tinsel from the counter, and anything else he could think of – and the tree really began to look very beautiful!

"I can make a star to go on the top of the tree," said the teddy bear, and he ran off to find some silver paper.

"And now don't any of you look," said the sailor, "because I'm going to wrap presents for you – yes, a present for every single one of you!"

The circus was practicing hard. There were two wind-up clowns in the toy shop, so they were exactly right for the circus. They could go head-over-heels very fast.

"We need some horses," said the black monkey, who was very busy. "Pink cat, stop prowling around the cakes, and see how many horses you can find."

The roly-poly man said he wanted to be a clown, so the teddy bear made him a clown's hat, and let him roll around the ring, knocking people over. Jack-out-of-his-Box jumped around and wiggled his head on his long neck. He was really very funny.

The pink cat borrowed some horses from the soldiers and the farm. She led them down to the circus ring.

Noah arrived with his animals from the ark. There were elephants, lions, tigers, and even kangaroos!

"It's going to be a GRAND circus!" said the pink cat. "Oh, hurry up and come, Christmas Day!"

Well, Christmas Day did come at last! The toys ran to one another, shouting "Merry Christmas! Merry Christmas!" at the tops of their voices.

The wind-up train whistled its loudest. The big bear
and the little bears pressed themselves in the middle and
growled. The music box began to play, and the rag doll
sat down at the toy piano and played a rollicking tune.

Nobody knew she could play, and they were
all very surprised. So was the rag doll.
She hadn't known either, and once
she had begun to play she couldn't
stop! So with the train's
whistle, the bears' growling,
the music box's tunes,
and the piano there
was a wonderful
noise.

The roly-poly man got so excited that he knocked over two of the horses, rolled on the monkey's tail, and spilled a jug of lemonade.

"Can't you stop rolling around and be still for a moment?" said the pink cat, keeping her tail well out of the way.

"I can't stand still," said the roly-poly man, "because I've got something very heavy at the bottom of me. It makes me wobble, but not fall over. I really will try to be good – but if you were as wobbly as I am you'd find it difficult, too."

The black monkey suddenly appeared dressed up in white trousers and a top hat! He carried a whip in his hand. He cracked it and made everyone jump.

Then the pink cat appeared, carrying a drum. She beat it – boom-diddy-boom-diddy-boom-boom-boom.

"The circus is about to begin!" shouted the black monkey and he cracked his whip again. "Step right up, everyone! The circus is about to begin!"

"Boom-diddy-boom-diddy-boom!" went the drum.

All the toys rushed for seats. The black monkey had arranged blocks of all sizes and shapes out of the block-boxes for seats, and there was room for everyone. The doll house dolls were allowed to be at the front because they were so small.

The skittles were so excited that they kept giggling and falling over.

"Quiet there! Settle down please!" shouted the monkey. "Pink cat, sound the drum again – the performers are about to march in."

The circus began. You should have seen it! The horses were splendid. They ran around the ring one way, and then turned and went the other way.

Then the clowns came on, with Jack and the roly-poly man. The roly-poly man rolled all over the place and knocked all the clowns over. Then the clowns tried to catch Jack, but they couldn't, of course, because Jack sprang away from them on his long spring. The toys almost cried with laughter.

The elephants were cheered when they came in. They waved their trunks in the air and trumpeted as loudly as they could. The lions and tigers came in and roared fiercely. The kangaroos jumped all around the ring and the bears walked in standing up on their hind legs.

All the toys clapped and cheered and stamped at the end, and said it was the very best circus in the world. The pink cat and the black monkey felt very proud, and they stood in the middle of the ring and bowed to everyone so many times that they made their backs ache.

"Now for the tea party!" called the doll with golden hair. "Come along! You must be very hungry, toys – hurry up and come to the party!"

What a wonderful tea party it was! There were little tables everywhere. In the middle of them were vases of flowers that the dolls had picked out of the dolls' hats that Miss Roundy kept in a box on a special shelf.

The tables were set with the cups and saucers and plates out of the boxes of toy tea sets. There was a tea-pot on each, full of lemonade to pour into the cups.

The cakes were lovely. There were fudge cakes, peppermints, chocolate cakes, all kinds of cookies, toffee sandwiches, jelly candy that wobbled like the roly-poly man, and, of course, the Christmas cake was the best thing of all.

"We've put it on a table by itself, because it's so big," said the golden-haired doll. "I hope there will be a slice for everybody. Light the candles, twin dolls."

The cake blazed up, all its tiny candles alight. It looked beautiful. The golden-haired doll had decorated it with icing. Everyone thought that was very clever.

The pink cat ate so much that she got fatter than ever. The captain of the soldiers lent the twin dolls his sharp sword to cut the cake. The roly-poly man rolled up to see them cutting it, and nearly got his head cut off!

When nobody could eat any more, and all the lemonade was drunk, the skittles cleared the tables. "We'll wash the dishes and put all the tea sets back in their boxes," they said. "The rest of you can play games."

So, while the skittles were busy, the toys played party games. They played blind man's buff, and the blindfolded pink cat caught the elephant from the Noah's Ark.

"Who can it be?" wondered the pink cat, feeling the elephant carefully. All the toys laughed, because of course, they knew who it was.

They played hunt the thimble, and nobody could see for a long time where the thimble was hidden. Then the wind-up sailor gave a scream.

"The captain of the soldiers is wearing it for a helmet – he is, he is!"

And so he was. He was sorry to give it up because he thought it was a very nice helmet.

The trains gave everyone rides, and so did the toy cars. Even the airplane said it would fly around the nursery once with everybody. The music box played hard for anyone who wanted to dance.

The roly-poly man made everyone laugh when he tried to dance with the rag doll. He rolled around so much that he knocked everyone off the floor.

They were all having such a good time. Then suddenly they noticed that all the candles on the Christmas tree were lighted!

"Oh, oh! It's time for the Christmas tree!" cried the toys, and they rushed over to it. "Isn't it pretty? Look at the star at the top!"

"Where's the wind-up sailor?" said the roly-poly man.

"Gone to get Santa Claus, he told me," said the rocking horse. "Do you suppose he meant it?"

And then, will you believe it, there came the noise of bells!

"Sleigh bells! It really is Santa Claus coming!" cried all the toys, and they rushed to the chimney. "He's coming! He's coming!"

Down the chimney came
a pair of legs – then a pair
of red pants – and then
with a jump, down on the
rug came a merry,
white-whiskered fellow,
whose red hood framed
his jolly red face.

"Santa Claus! You've come, you've come!" shouted the toys, and dragged him to the tree.

"Wait a bit – I want my sack. It's just a little way up the chimney," said Santa Claus. So the big teddy bear got it. It was a nice big bumpy-looking sack.

"Merry Christmas, toys," said Santa Claus. He was a very nice *little* Santa Claus, not much bigger than the dolls. The toys were glad. They would have been afraid of a great big one.

"Merry Christmas!" sang out everyone. Then Santa Claus undid his bag. Oh, what a lot of things he had! There were ribbons and necklaces for the dolls, candy for the soldiers, chocolates for the Noah's Ark animals, and balls, made of red holly berries, for the toy animals. Nobody had been forgotten. It was wonderful.

Santa Claus handed out all the presents, beaming happily. Then he took a few presents from under the tree.

"These are special presents for the people who tried to make your Christmas so nice," he said. "Presents for the golden-haired doll and the twin dolls – and for the black monkey and the pink cat – here you are, special little presents for being kind and good."

"But what about the wind-up sailor?" said the rocking horse, at once. "He did the tree, you know. Have you forgotten him?"

"Where is he?" said Santa Claus.

Well, dear me, he wasn't there! Would you believe it?

"I saw him last," said the rocking horse. "He said he was going to get you, Santa Claus. *Didn't* he bring you?"

"Well, I'm here, aren't I?" said Santa Claus, and he laughed. "Dear me – it's sad there's no present for the wind-up sailor, but I don't think he'll mind at all."

The toys had opened all their presents. Somewhere a clock struck twelve. Midnight! Dear dear, how very late!

The twin dolls yawned loudly, and that made everyone yawn, too.

"We'd better clean up and go to bed," said the golden-haired doll. "Or we shall fall asleep on our feet, and that would never do."

So they cleaned up, and in the middle of it all Santa Claus disappeared. Nobody saw him go. The pink cat said she saw him go into the doll house, but he wasn't there when she looked.

Somebody else was, though – the wind-up sailor! The pink cat dragged him out.

"Here's the sailor!" she cried. "Here he is! Sailor, you missed Santa Claus – oh what a shame!"

But, you know, he didn't! He was there all the time. Have you guessed? He was Santa Claus, of course, all dressed up. He had climbed up the chimney when nobody was looking. Wasn't he clever?

"You were Santa Claus!" cried the golden-haired doll, and she hugged him hard. "You're a dear!"

"Yes, you are," shouted the rocking horse. "That was the best part of all, when Santa Claus came. We were so sad there was no present for you. But you will have one – you will, you will!"

And he did. The toys threaded a whole lot of red holly berries together and made him the finest necklace he had ever had. Look at him wearing it. Doesn't he look pleased?

Miss Roundy will never guess all that the toys did in her toy shop that Christmas Day, will she? If you ever meet her, you can tell her. I wish I'd been there to see it all, don't you?